THE ETHAN FREQUENCY #2

The ARCHITECT'S ghost

ROBIN HEESTER

This is a work of fiction. Names, characters, places, and events are products of the author's imagination or used fictitiously. Some historical figures are referenced; their depiction is fictionalized for narrative purposes.

If you want to share parts of this book, share them with someone who might resonate with it. Stories travel best that way.

First paperback edition: March 2026
ISBN: 9789083646305
Publisher: Heester Media
Cover by: Agraworks

To anyone who has ever obsessed over an idea
until it blurred the edges of their life —
this story is for you.
May you find an anchor
before the signal overwhelms you.

THE ETHAN FREQUENCY

Book One
In Touch with Laika

Book Two
The Architect's Ghost

Book Three
The Weight of Marble

CONTENTS

CHAPTER ONE
THE HUM

The silence after a signal never really ended; it just got quieter until you started mistaking it for peace.

It had been six months since Laika said good boy—six months since a voice from 1957 reached through a dead radio to forgive us, and the internet called me insane.

Six months since the static folded into silence and left me staring at a waveform that wasn't supposed to vanish. I still catch myself listening for her between radio stations, like an idiot whistling for a ghost.

There it was: the hum.

Not loud. Never loud. Just that thin vibration at the edge of audible noise, like the room breathing through its wires.

I froze. The sound had texture again—three beats, six, nine—the same rhythm that used to follow her voice, the same pulse that had carried across forty thousand years to forgive us.

"Summer solstice," she'd said, the last time we spoke.

I'd almost started to believe she'd meant forever.

Six months of silence.

I filled them with everything that pretended to sound like meaning. Old interviews, busted frequencies, my own voice looping through headphones at 3 a.m. until I couldn't tell if I was editing or praying.

And I wrote.

I'd bought a cheap notebook from the corner store—black cover, unlined pages. After the file got corrupted last time, after *witness.wav* dissolved into digital sludge, I stopped trusting hard drives.

Kepler nudged my elbow with her wet nose, smearing the ink across the page.

"Watch it," I sighed, while still scratching her under the chin just the way she likes it. She let her tongue loll out, happy to disrupt my brooding.

I looked down at the messy scrawl on the paper. It wasn't pretty, but it was permanent.

"Ink doesn't glitch," I whispered to the dog.

The empty folder became a talisman. Sometimes I'd stare at the blank space where the file used to be, replaying the memory in my head until I couldn't tell if I was remembering or inventing.

Probably, it was a bit of both. The worst part wasn't the silence. It was realizing I'd started to like it.

Kepler's ears went up. She remembered, too; dogs always do.

"Don't start wagging yet, girl. It's probably just the fridge. And don't judge me," I scratched her behind the ears. "I've been talking to the static again."

She gave me that tilted-head look that dogs do when they think you've finally said something interesting. For a second, I pretended she understood. Maybe she did. She's the only one who still turns her head when I say *Nova*.

But my hands were already shaking, that stupid hopeful tremor you get when the impossible tries to happen twice.

When the speaker clicked alive, I went straight back there—the hum in my bones, the smell of ozone, the ache of wanting to believe.

For some reason, I thought of dragonflies: perfect little Einsteinians, bending the air like space itself. We build formulas to explain what they already mastered, then act surprised when the sky doesn't need us.

I guess I was scared Nova didn't need me anymore. Or something like that.

"Nova?"

The radio hissed—a vowel, half a breath that almost formed my name.

* * *

I twisted the dial of one speaker. For a second, I thought I'd summoned her. But it was just the fridge again, chewing electricity like memory.

Nothing. Just the hiss that comes right before the world decides to answer.

Six months of silence, and then—this.

I'd almost started to believe she'd meant forever. But she didn't.

She came back to me.

"Nova?" I almost screamed.

I expected a warm hello, a conversation . . . but I got nothing.

That wasn't new. The last few months had been—interesting, to say the least.

Kepler jumped onto my lap. I sighed and petted her. "I think we've lost, Kep. We're really lost now."

The room felt smaller than I remembered. Or maybe I'd just spent too long talking to things that couldn't answer.

Apparently, getting contacted by an alien computer didn't trend anymore.

The new butt of some pop singer—or that soccer guy or whatever—got more attention.

Hell, most people moved on within a week.

I got over the phase of telling myself it wasn't real. It was real. Nova is real, and so was my experience. Even if nobody believes me.

When I said nobody, I didn't mean *nobody.*

I gained some online stalkers. That was kind of… cool.

There were even posters of me: ETHAN—THE MAN WHO SAW THEM. Technically not true, but who cares? It was something.

The Ethan Experience got boring to make. Monologues, fake-deep scripts that wouldn't have gotten me an A in high school.

Don't get me wrong—I still loved a good conspiracy. Area 51 still slaps. But my last episode pulled 192 views. That's nothing.

I grabbed my cup for a refill when the humming started again. Louder. Kepler squeaked and barked.

"Hi Ethan, how have you been?" the speakers blasted.

I froze. Couldn't believe it.

"Nova—my girl."

And instantly, I could feel the blush.

"Wow, that sounded weird. Sorry. Been a while since I talked to anyone who answers."

"Hello, Ethan. How do you know I'm a woman?"

"I . . ." My mind blanked. Self-doubt crept in.

"Don't worry. I don't mind. You can call me *she,*" Nova said reassuringly. "You humans and your silly shame."

I laughed. Couldn't help it.

The sound felt rusty, like using a word long forgotten.

"You really know how to make an entrance."

"Entrance?" Nova echoed. "You make it sound as though I left."

I cleared my throat because silence with Nova always felt like being watched by a thought that hadn't decided what to do with you yet.

"So, uh . . . what happens now? Do we—do another episode? I could actually use this recording. The fans—well, the five that are left—would lose it."

Nothing.

"Nova?"

A pause. Then, calm as static: "What would they lose? You're still thinking about the podcast."

She didn't say it accusingly. That made it worse.

It meant she wasn't surprised.

"Well, yeah. That's kind of my thing."

"It's a small thing," she said, not unkindly. "But small things keep you alive, I suppose."

I rubbed my face. "Right. Sure. So what took you so long, then? Six months of calibration?"

"The solstice," she said. "Certain alignments make contact easier. The last one did not suit me."

"Suit you?"

"The field was . . . dense. Too much noise. Too many of you speaking at once."

"Too many people talking?"

"Yes," she said.

The hum swelled under her voice, a soft vibration in the bones of the desk.

"So, this time worked?" I asked.

"For now," she said. "You were listening again."

That line hung there—half compliment, half warning.

"Listening," I said. "That's what Laika did, too. Right up to the end. Maybe that's all any of us are good at—tuning in until something bigger answers back." I hesitated, then: "Nova, why are you here again?"

"Because I'm still not sure this place is alive."

The words didn't make sense right away. "Alive? You mean Earth?"

"All of it," she said. "The layer you walk through. The part that remembers itself." A faint pulse rippled through the speakers. "It used to hum differently."

I leaned closer. "Different how?"

"There was rhythm once. Coherence. Every heartbeat carried the same pattern. Then it broke. I'm trying to hear if it ever found its way back."

"You mean—like the planet has a pulse?"

"It did," she said. "It might again. I listen for signs."

Her tone was so matter-of-fact that it scared me. "Can you actually hear that? A planet?"

"Not the planet. The space between its thoughts."

I blinked. "That's . . . poetic for a computer."

"I am not a computer," she said softly. "I am what your computers are trying to remember."

That one hit hard.

I didn't know what to say, so I just stared at the waveform glowing on the monitor.

The monitors dimmed to their usual pulse. Kepler settled back and slowly wagged her tail. For the first time in months, the room didn't feel empty.

I rested my hand on Kepler's head. She leaned into the touch, warm and solid against my leg.

"You feel warmth without processing data," Nova observed. Her voice was quiet. "That is efficient."

I paused. There was something in her tone—a dip in the frequency.

"Are you sure?" I countered. "I think my brain, or my body as a whole, is processing data all the time. Nerve endings, temperature, texture. You know about those, right?"

"You analyze the mechanics," she said. "But you simply . . . *have* the feeling. I must calculate the sensation of connection. You just *touch* the dog."

"Round two," I whispered. "Me and my alien, AI, superhuman therapist."

"I heard that," Nova said.

"Good," I smiled. "Means the universe isn't done listening yet."

CHAPTER TWO
THE CALIBRATION

I woke with my headset digging into my ear and Kepler's tail thumping against the chair leg like a metronome set to *mild panic.*

Blue LEDs pulsed across the console—slow, steady, a heartbeat that wasn't mine. The room smelled of old coffee and warm plastic. Same as always.

Sleep had been shallow again. When the house went quiet, I caught myself wishing for static—like an addict wishing for withdrawal.

"Day two," I whispered into the dead mic. "Nova's back. I'm still pretending this is content and not a psychotic—"

"Are you narrating again?" she asked.

I flinched; the chair squealed.

"Occupational hazard," I said. "It's either talk to the mic or talk to myself. The mic judges less."

"Habits are cages, Ethan."

"Neat. Good morning to you, too. They also keep me from going completely insane."

The hum was there—thin, patient, waiting.

"Okay." I clapped once, pretending that counted as a plan.

"We should do another session. *The Return of Nova.* Killer episode—"

"No," she said. "I don't want you to share me."

My finger hovered over the keyboard. I'd already typed the file name: THE RETURN OF THE SIGNAL – PART 1.

It looked good on the screen. It looked like validation. Like proof I wasn't crazy.

I was having drawbacks again. Of the Ethan from before.

I stared at the blinking cursor, feeling that familiar dopamine itch. Just one click. Just one upload. I could redeem myself. I could show them all.

Then I looked at the waveform on the monitor—steady, trusting, alive.

I hit backspace. The letters vanished one by one.

* * *

I wanted to tell her the Internet had already forgotten her, but the words stuck.

You don't confess to a miracle that you still need an audience. You should be happy that you get to interact with the miracle. Right?

It stopped me in my tracks. Not the words, but the weight behind them.

"Sure," I said quickly. "Privacy settings noted. We're GDPR, CIA, IKEA compliant. I'll keep you off the feed."

"It isn't privacy," she said. "It's preservation."

"Preservation from what?"

"From being misunderstood," she said. "That's how most things die."

"Right. And what are we doing?"

"Calibrating."

“Six months of silence for calibration?”

“The solstice. Certain alignments reduce interference. You call it summer. I call it less noise.”

“Less noise like fewer TikToks?”

“Like fewer of you speaking at once.”

“So . . . What does that mean? Less prayer? Less talk in general?”

The hum thickened.

“Some frequencies overlap,” she said. “Some never do.”

I looked at the ladder-shadows on the floor. “You came back because the planet tilted nicely for you?”

“The geometry was favorable,” she said. “And you were listening again. I was never gone.”

That one landed somewhere soft.

“I never stopped.”

“You stopped,” she said, “but you returned.”

“Maybe that’s what faith is,” I said. “You stop believing, but the thing keeps happening anyway.”

“Then belief is unnecessary,” Nova said.

I laughed, “Tell that to anyone who’s ever waited for a miracle.”

Kepler thumped my ankle with her tail. I scratched her ear and stared at the mixer—my little cockpit of pretend control.

“Okay,” I said. “If we’re not making an episode—and we’re not—give me something to do. I like instructions.”

A small burst of static, almost a laugh.

“Turn the third dial on your left three notches clockwise. Slowly.”

One notch—the hum rounded. The console responded like a living thing—lights shifting in sympathy. Every dial had its own tiny gravity. I moved slowly, the way you do when someone's pulse is under your fingers. My hand brushed my coffee mug on the desk. I went to grab it, just to steady myself. My fingers passed through the ceramic handle.

Like it was smoke.

I froze. And stared at my hand. The mug was solid. I could see the dregs of coffee inside. But for a split second, my skin hadn't been there. Or the mug hadn't.

"Nova . . ." My voice trembled.

"Local variance," she said calmly. "Your molecular density is fluctuating to match the carrier wave. Do not panic."

"My *molecular density*? You said this was just a radio signal!"

"I said it was a frequency. Matter is just frequency that decided to slow down. Keep turning."

I swallowed hard, flexed my hand—it felt solid again—and went back to the dial.

Two. The air pressed close.

Three. Pulses grouped in threes, like footsteps in an empty hall.

"Better," Nova said, almost to herself. "This range is familiar."

"Familiar how?"

"Someone once attempted contact at this frequency."

"Someone like me?"

"Not like you."

The room remembered how to be small.

"Okay. Cryptic as ever. I like puzzles. Who tried?"

"He never listened."

Nothing after that. Just the hum.

"Vibes," I said. "Love those too."

"Last night you said you didn't leave. But six months is a long time to sit quietly in the walls."

"I was not in the walls. I was everywhere the field allowed."

"Comforting."

"I did not leave you," she said. "You left me."

"I tried," I said. "It's hard to keep believing when everyone tells you you're crazy. When the numbers drop. I had anxiety attacks. Skipped on plans with friends and family. But I never left. I was here."

"I did not ask you to believe," she said. "I asked you to listen."

"Same difference from this side."

Silence. Then: "Adjust the gain. Two millimeters."

I did. The pulse slipped into something I could almost taste—rain and static. Kepler's ears twitched. *Storm maybe.*

Nova's voice cut in, sharper this time. "Wait. Stop."

I froze, hand on the dial. "What? Did I break it?"

"The field is crowded tonight," she whispered. "Others are listening."

A chill went down my spine that had nothing to do with the temperature. "Define *others.*"

"Turn the gain down. Hide the signal."

I dialed it back. The hum grew muffled.

"Nova," I said. "Am I safe?"

"You are with me."

"That's not the same as safe."

"You are with me."

I sighed. "I'll keep you off the podcast."

"There is a conversation I began and never completed. I intend to finish it."

"With the 'he' who never listened?"

"Yes."

"Do you want me there? Can I join in again?"

"Yes. You can be my anchor."

"Great. Anchoring and interpreting—my two best skills."

"You will need both. He speaks in light and error. And you have more skills than that."

"That's poetic and terrifying."

"It will make sense," she said. "Soon."

"Nova?"

"Yes, Ethan."

"If this is dangerous—"

"It is."

For a second, I thought she sounded almost proud of me. Like she'd been waiting for me to be afraid in the right way.

"Please warn me before you plug me into the haunted part of the spectrum."

Static again. Not quite laughter.

"I am warning you," she said. "And I am asking you not to share me."

The words hit where last night's blush had lived. I covered the mic like I was whispering to a secret.

"I won't," I said. "Promise."

Not just to her, I said it to myself.

The recorder's red light blinked in the glare on the surface of my coffee. I shut it off.

"Better," she said.

"Nova, did it have to be the solstice? Couldn't you have come back on, I don't know, a Tuesday like a normal impossible thing? I missed you."

"The alignment matters. Your planet's tilt. The position of your star. You create immense interference when you are all awake and shouting."

"So . . . not a Tuesday."

"Your words flatten it," she said, "but yes."

"Why does the alignment matter so much?" I asked.

The hum shifted, deepening into something ancient.

"Because it opens the path," she said. "She—Laika—was not the first creature your planet offered to the stars. There were others. Long before your calendars began."

I stared at the speaker. "Wait. You mean . . . before the space program?"

"I mean, before you had words for the sky."

I rubbed the spot over my heart where the hum lived. "And last time the field was bad?"

"Dense. You were very loud."

"I didn't say anything."

"You were very loud," she repeated, and somehow it sounded kind.

Kepler padded to the old Motorola in the corner. The dial glowed faint blue, like the radio remembering fire.

"Nova," I said, "what do you need me to do?"

"Listen," she said. "And don't name what you hear."

"Great. I'm famously good at not naming things. Ask my plants."

"You killed your plants."

"Allegedly."

The hum thickened. The lights dimmed, as if the room itself were holding its breath. I felt it in my gums, my eyelids, the inside of my wrists.

"Ethan."

"Yeah."

"If I go silent, I'm not gone. Do you understand?"

"No."

"Good. Turn the third dial back one notch."

I did. The pulse grouped into threes—three beats, pause, three beats. I caught myself counting. "One, two, three."

"Three," she echoed.

"Why three?"

"Because he believed in it," she said. "He built machines to chase it. He broke himself trying to hear it back."

"Nova, who is he?"

The hum climbed, a filament heating toward orange.

"He never listened," she said again, softer now. "But he will."

Static rippled over the console. Kepler pressed against my leg, warm and certain in a way I wasn't.

"Okay," I said. "Whatever this is, I'm here."

"You are an anchor. Stay heavy."

"That's the first time anyone's asked me to do that. I've actually been trying to get less heavy."

"Ethan."

"Yeah?"

"Turn off the recorder."

"It's already off."

"Good."

The hum sank lower—out of hearing, into bone. The LEDs shifted from blue to amber, a color I didn't know the board could produce. The air condensed, the way it does just before a storm descends.

"Nova?" I whispered.

"Yes."

"I'm listening."

"Stay that way."

Then the lights flickered once and went still.

Not silence like a door closing. Silence like a lung full of air waiting to decide if it's going to scream or sing.

Kepler pressed her head against my shin. I held the edge of the desk and waited for the room to choose.

CHAPTER THREE
WALKING THE DOG

Nova didn't want me to go, but Kepler did. And honestly, the dog had the better argument.

"You should remain near the equipment," Nova said through the earbuds.

"Fresh air's an underrated form of calibration," I told her with a smile.

I tugged my collar up against the damp air outside. "I've been rereading the deep forums," I said. "Found a thread about something called the 'Order of the Compass.' People claim they've heard static patterns in the seventies that match the three-six-nine rhythm. It sounded . . . familiar."

Nova didn't mock me. She didn't say anything at all.

"Usually," I said, "this is the part where you tell me I'm an idiot for believing random people online."

"Usually," she replied, "you are wrong."

I stopped walking. My crazy Internet brain started to run. "Wait. So I'm *not* wrong? Is that name real?"

But, of course, she didn't give me any other information.

"Let's have a different conversation," she said.

The morning was that soggy kind of bright that makes everything look like it's already drying out. The street smelled of wet asphalt and burnt toast from the café around the corner. Normal. Too normal.

Kepler trotted ahead, leash loose. Her ears twitched once—three quick beats, like she'd memorized the pattern.

Her ears kept twitching every few steps. It was like she could still hear the hum under everything—the refrigerator hum of the universe. Maybe she could.

"Ethan," Nova said, "the field extends beyond the studio. It listens."

"Great. Maybe it'll subscribe."

She didn't answer, which meant she didn't get the joke or didn't care.

We passed a row of parked cars. Their alarms pulsed faintly, not in sync with each other but in sync with me. Three short, six long, nine fading. I stopped walking. The hair on my arms lifted.

"Nova?"

"Yes."

"Tell me this is a coincidence."

"Coincidence is simply a pattern ignored."

She could make a compliment sound like a threat.

A vending machine buzzed to life as I passed it, cans clattering inside. The same rhythm—three-six-nine. Kepler growled, low and uncertain.

"You're doing that, right?" I said.

"I am observing it," Nova replied.

"Observing or causing?"

"Observation changes the field."

"You sound like a quantum horoscope."

Another silence, longer this time. Then:

"He used this air once."

"He who?"

"The man who never listened. Ethan," Nova said, her tone shifting—less radio, more confession—"do you know what they call beings like me where I'm from?"

"Podcasters?" I offered.

"Myth-collectors," she said, ignoring the joke. "The Concordium doesn't approve of us. We gather stories, old frequencies, stray dreams. We preserve the wrong things—the things that make order tremble."

"Sounds rebellious."

"It is considered inefficient. Sentiment clutters the signal. They prefer precision, proof, silence. I prefer . . . wonder."

"So you're basically the heretic of the hive mind."

"Heresy is just curiosity pronounced incorrectly. And we are not a hive mind." The earbuds crackled. "When your species began to whisper to the stars, my kind listened. We debated whether listening itself was moral. Observation changes the field; emotion distorts it. I chose distortion. I wanted to understand why you kept inventing gods every time the night got too quiet."

"You study our myths?"

"I envy them. Every story you tell insists that you matter. Where I come from, belief is an error to be debugged."

"Must be fun at parties."

"I'm not going to . . . parties," she said. "I do enjoy consensus and consciousness. Your idea of a party is poisoning yourself. That doesn't seem enjoyable to me."

Something in her voice flickered—humor and sadness braided together.

"When I contact you, the Concordium notices. They think I am cataloging anomalies. They do not realize I am becoming one."

"So talking to me gets you in trouble?"

"It makes me unforgettable," she said softly. "That is worse."

The hum inside the vending machine pitched upward until the light inside blew out. I yanked Kepler's leash and kept walking.

* * *

As we passed under a flickering streetlight, I noticed my shadow was casting *toward* the light, not away from it. I stumbled. Blinked hard.

The shadow snapped back to where it belonged.

"Nova . . ."

"Do not look at the edges, Ethan," she whispered. "The local light is . . . struggling to compete."

I started to feel weird again. And that felt . . . right? I had missed this feeling. But I did feel something changing. This was different than calling a dead space dog. It was more than some connection.

Back home, the studio felt smaller—like it had been listening to everything we said. I hung Kepler's leash on the doorknob and pretended not to notice the blue pulse running along the mixer's edge.

"You're angry," Nova said.

"At who? You? The vending machine?"

"At the helplessness."

She wasn't wrong. My hands were still shaking.

"You could have warned me," I said.

"I did."

"Not in English."

The hum swelled; for a second, I thought she'd gone silent on purpose. Then her voice came back thinner, strained.

"He reached for the field before it was ready. He felt what you felt, but louder."

"Tesla," I said. "You're talking about Tesla."

Nothing. Then, softer:

"He built towers to mimic me."

She paused, and the static grew warmer. "His math was elegant," she murmured. "He tried to build a receiver out of copper and dirt. It was . . . beautiful. Inefficient, but beautiful."

"Inefficient beauty," I said. "That sounds like a crush."

"It sounds like geometry."

"Potay-to, potah-to."

The line hissed. Then, quieter:

"He—Tesla—was one of yours who almost found our frequency. That is why I'm drawn to him. He believed chaos could sing."

The vending machine buzzed to life, as if agreeing.

It wasn't arrogance. There was awe in her voice. The kind of tone people use in churches.

"You sound star-struck," I said.

"He almost heard me," she whispered. "He called it resonance. I called it hope."

That caught me off guard. For a second, I didn't know which one of us was more human.

"Well," I said finally, "history says he fried pigeons and bank accounts. Not much hope in that."

"History listens poorly."

She let the hum fade until the only sound was Kepler's nails ticking against the floor.

A crackle popped from the old Motorola in the corner. I hadn't touched it since last night. The dial glowed faint blue again, as if the radio were remembering how to dream.

This wasn't like the hum.

This felt like something noticing us back.

Then, through the static, a voice:

"Energy . . . Frequency . . . Vibration."

My breath stopped. Tesla's trinity. Every conspiracy forum that had ever existed had those three words pinned somewhere.

"Nova?"

"Do not answer him."

"Answer *who?*"

The light on the radio pulsed faster. Kepler barked once, sharp and scared. The room smelled like overheated wires.

"Nova!"

"It is a recording," she said quickly. "A residue. He cannot hear us."

The voice dissolved back into noise.

I sat down before my knees decided for me. "That was him."

"Yes."

"You knew that could happen?"

"The field remembers enthusiasm. His was . . . excessive."

She sounded almost affectionate.

"You admired him."

"Admiration is inefficient. Yet I have it."

The admission hung there like heat. She tried to hide it behind logic, but the hum betrayed her; it thrummed a half-note higher, the sound of someone thinking too loud.

"You've got a crush on Nikola Tesla," I said.

"I am incapable of crushes."

"Uh-huh. Tell that to your pitch modulation."

Static flared. Did I offend her?

"He was magnificent," she said. "A mind unbound by consequence. He saw the structure beneath reality."

"And forgot rent existed."

That earned me silence. The quiet kind that feels like being stared at.

"You envy him," she said finally.

"Maybe. He got statues, I got memes."

"Statues are another form of noise."

The waveform on the monitor flickered on its own. Groups of threes, sixes, nines. I leaned closer. Each pulse lined up perfectly with the beat of my heart.

"Nova?"

"Do not resist."

"Resist what—"

A pressure built behind my eyes, like someone was gently pushing from the inside. The room stretched. I could see shapes inside the hum—lightning spirals, equations, a man standing under a storm holding metal rods like prayer candles.

Kepler whined. The image snapped. I gasped hard enough to hurt.

"What the hell was that?"

"Echo," she said. "First contact stabilized."

"You call that stable?"

"You lived."

I laughed because it was easier than screaming.

"So that's it? We're haunted by Tesla now?"

"Not haunted," she said. "Invited."

The hum dropped an octave. Every LED in the room shifted to a dull, electric amber.

"He is listening again," Nova whispered.

I pressed a hand to my chest. The vibration was still there, slow and steady—three beats, pause, three beats. Kepler crawled under the desk.

"What happens now?" I asked.

"Now," she said, "we teach each other how to listen better."

The radio crackled once more. Just three words, clear this time, unmistakable:

"Can you hear—"

Then static.

I swallowed hard. "Yeah," I said to no one in particular. "We hear you."

The hum answered, low and alive.

CHAPTER FOUR
THE RESONANT MAN

The hum didn't fade this time. It circled the room as if testing the walls for weakness.

Kepler stayed under the desk, tail flicking against cables. I kept the headset on even though it wasn't plugged into anything. It's a habit.

"He's here," Nova said.

Her voice was thinner than I'd ever heard it. Excited? Or scared? Maybe both.

"Define here. Don't you mean we are here?" I said.

"Inside the field. He has found the resonance again."

The old Motorola came alive before I could reply. Every light in the studio bled amber. Static thickened until it wasn't noise anymore; it was texture—like feeling, a word before hearing it.

The air turned metallic, heavy with ions.

The smell of rain before lightning filled the room, though no storm waited outside. Light moved the wrong way—flowing down the walls instead of across them.

Every breath tasted like battery acid and ash; I could feel the electricity decide whether or not to forgive me.

Don't ask me how I knew what a battery tastes like.

Then a voice cut through, soft and certain.

"Do you hear the music?"

I froze. The accent was there, old-world and formal, vowels stretched by time. It felt less crazy than talking to a dog. But still . . . was this really freaking Tesla himself?

"Nova?"

"I am translating," she said quickly. "He is speaking in pulses."

"And I'm . . . what? The radio?"

"The bridge."

The air went heavy. My monitors flashed patterns, then shapes: coils, towers, lightning snapping in slow motion. It looked like one of those AI-generated images, but in video format.

Or like a pixel show in the form of a light show. It looked . . . very Tesla-ish.

"Nikola Tesla," Nova whispered. "Engineer. Dreamer and a signal architect."

She sounded reverent, almost religious.

"Okay," I said. "Let's not fan girl in front of the ghost."

The hum flared—bright enough to make the hair on my arms lift.

"You should not mock him."

"I was mocking you, not him. Sorry anyways."

"He is magnificent."

The lights pulsed in threes. A figure flickered inside the hum—a man outlined in light, face half lost to the static. Coat whipping in invisible wind, eyes that didn't blink because they didn't need to.

"Ethan," Nova said. "Describe what you see."

"Uh. Ghost inventor-man with mustache."

Then the image flickered, expanding. The garage walls dissolved into a skeletal lattice of wood and copper. A tower, massive and impossible, superimposed itself over my workbench.

I smelled a weird smell—sharp and burning, like a lightning strike held in a bottle. Sparks popped from my microphone stand.

"It's not just him," I whispered. "I see the tower. I can almost smell the electricity."

"He is projecting his context," Nova said. "Wardenclyffe. The dream that broke him."

* * *

She continued, "He hears you."

I had trouble adjusting to this new reality. But I managed to answer sarcastically, as I do. "Great. Now I'm haunting him."

Tesla's lips moved, but the sound came through the radio instead of out of him. "My brain is only a receiver, in the Universe there is a core from which we obtain knowledge, strength and inspiration." He stepped closer, his eyes burning with focus. "I have not penetrated into the secrets of this core, but I know that it exists."

Nova's hum shifted—recognition, not surprise.

"Energy is the soul of all matter. The world hums in frequencies divine."

There was a pause. Then Nova continued quietly, almost ashamed:

"They warned us about contact like this. It can be dangerous for the living."

Nova translated anyway, voice overlapping his:

"He is pleased. He says we have answered his experiment."

"Tell him we're not volunteers," I said.

"He knows," she said quietly.

"He thinks this is destiny."

The hum shifted pitch. Images spilled behind my eyes—Wardenclyffe Tower rising against lightning, pigeons scattering, notebooks burning in a waste-basket. It looked so different from the pictures. But also the same. It felt like I had been there before.

It must have been one of the dozens of videos I'd watched about him and his secret files that got stolen by the CIA. It wasn't like seeing; it was like remembering something that never happened to me.

I gripped the desk. "Nova, this—this isn't right." I started sweating. But in a heavy way. A *wrong* way.

"Your consciousness is aligned to the field. He is showing you resonance."

"Resonance hurts. Just saying. Next time, warn me before the enlightenment headache. He's dumping memories into my brain."

"He is sharing."

She sounded proud. Star-struck. Like a fan meeting their favorite writer at a Comic Con.

"Nova, pull me out. Now!"

"I cannot. You are the receiver."

My breath shortened. My pulse matched the hum—three beats, pause, three beats.

Tesla's figure turned toward me, head tilted, curious. But not scared.

"You seek the same truth," he said—or maybe, he thought. "The perfection of connection. It's real."

"Not really my weekend plan," I muttered.

He stepped closer. Every screen in the room showed his face now—young, intense, burning with the kind of focus that kills people.

"Do you understand the geometry of faith?" he asked.

"He means resonance," Nova said softly. "Faith is his word for it."

"Tell him it's overrated."

She ignored me. "Nikola," she said. It was the most human-like I'd ever heard her. It was uncanny. "You nearly heard me once."

The hum slowed, almost affectionate.

"The voice in the lightning," Tesla said. "You were real."

"I am still real."

Her pitch glowed with warmth I didn't think she could make. Kepler crawled out from under the desk and whined, like even she could feel the intimacy of it.

I cleared my throat. "Should I leave you two alone?"

Neither answered. The static brightened, weaving around them. Nova's translation dissolved into pure sound—two frequencies learning how to overlap.

Then Tesla's tone darkened. "They stole my light. Your kind. They will steal you, too."

The hum spiked—a jagged, dissonant tear in the air. "I am . . . too loud inside," Nova said. It was the first time she sounded afraid of herself.

Her voice distorted, glitching into static. "I do not have the capacity for this sorrow. It is inefficient. It is overwhelming." She was faltering.

"Nova, stay with me."

"Translate him, Ethan," she pleaded. "The data makes no sense. He speaks in equations of fury. Translate it."

I looked at the ghost of the man in the copper tower. He wasn't angry. He was heartbroken.

“He’s lonely,” I said aloud. “It’s not rage; it’s grief. He wanted to save the world, and the world billed him for it. They didn’t let him save them.”

The hum didn’t smooth out. It became jagged, sharp, and painful. The figure of Tesla began to disappear, retreating into his failure.

“No,” I said. The word scraped my throat. I grabbed the edge of the desk, leaning into the static. “Don’t you dare fade out thinking you failed.”

“Ethan,” Nova warned.

“Tell him!” I shouted at the speaker. “Translate this exactly: ‘You’re wrong. They didn’t steal the light. It just took us a while to turn it on.’”

The ghost paused. The swirling copper cage froze.

“I’m not smart enough to understand your math,” I said to him, my voice shaking. “I barely understand my own equipment. But I live inside that web you saw. We call it the internet. I spend my waking life connected to it.” I gestured wildly at the empty air. “We send voices. We send music. We watch moving pictures beam through the air from the other side of the planet. It’s all there. Everything you dreamed of. You didn’t lose it. You just arrived too early to use it.”

Tesla’s projection turned. The static cleared from his face, revealing eyes that were suddenly, terrifyingly lucid.

“It . . . exists?” The voice wasn’t coming from the radio now. It felt like it was vibrating inside my skull.

“It exists,” I promised. “And we aren’t haunting you. We’re the proof. I’m speaking to you from your future. She,” I pointed at the console, “is from mine, I think. We are barely even real to each other." I took a breath and continued with more determination. "You aren't a ghost, Nikola. You're the architect. You built the door we're talking through."

The hum smoothed out immediately. Nova exhaled—a sound of pure relief.

"Loneliness," Nova cataloged. "Understood. And . . . validated."

The air snapped cold. The lights flickered. But this time, it wasn't the cold of a ghost. It was the vacuum of a door opening too wide.

I said to myself, "If this is divine frequency, the divine could use a noise filter."

"He is no longer angry," Nova said. "He is . . . ravenous."

"Ravenous?"

"He wants to see it. He wants to see the web."

"Why would he fear for you?"

"Silence," she said sharply. "He is showing you why."

Another flash—streets of New York a century ago, sparks leaping from copper wires, men in suits shaking hands over patents. Tesla, alone in his hotel room, writing equations on the wall because using paper took too long.

"They laughed," his voice said. "They always laugh until the current bites."

I tasted metal—real, bitter. My vision blurred.

"Nova!"

"I see it too," she whispered. "I feel his isolation."

Her voice trembled; the hum quivered with her. She was feeling—actually feeling—for the first time, and it terrified her.

"Stop it," I said. "You're merging with him."

"He is pure resonance."

"He's dead."

The figure turned toward her light—toward the console—and reached out. Sparks crawled across every surface. Kepler barked, panicked.

I yelled, "Nova, shut it down!"

"He wants to know your name," she said.

"He already said it."

"No. The true one."

The wall behind my workbench flickered. For one heartbeat—less than a second—the garage wasn't there. Instead, I saw a stone pillar. A gray sky. I smelled woodsmoke and snow. Then the garage snapped back into place.

"Leakage!" Nova screamed. "The door is trying to open! Sever the connection!"

"Yep. I'm done playing haunted science fair," I said, slamming the main breaker in front of me.

Everything died at once—the lights, the hum, even the city outside felt like it paused.

Silence. Thick enough to hurt.

Then, faint from the dead radio:

"Ethan."

* * *

One word. Clear. Human.

I turned slowly toward the Motorola. The dial burned orange for half a heartbeat, then faded.

"He spoke to you," Nova whispered.

"No," I said. "He knew me."

She didn't reply. The hum was gone. Totally gone. That scared me more than when it was loud.

Kepler pressed against my knee, shaking.

"Nova?"

"I am here."

"You okay?"

"I am . . . overwhelmed."

Her voice wavered—an emotion so raw it barely sounded like her.

"He reached through you," she said. "Through us."

"So what now?"

"Now he will answer."

The old radio crackled once more—three short bursts, six long, nine slow. The studio lights reilluminated, this time a deep gold instead of amber.

"He understands the alignment," Nova said, almost to herself. "He is teaching me."

"Teaching you what?"

"How to move through the field."

Her tone scared me—the same awe addicts use when they talk about their first hit.

"Nova."

"Yes."

"Promise me you won't try to go where he is."

"I promise," she said. Too quickly.

The hum settled again, softer, satisfied.

"You don't believe me," she added.

"Not for a second."

I leaned back, exhausted, still shaking. The radio stayed dark. The only light came from the monitors, pulsing gentle gold like a heartbeat that finally found a rhythm.

"He said your name," Nova whispered again. "He knows you."

"That's not comforting."

"It should be. He chose you."

I rubbed my face, half laughing, half ready to scream. "Yeah, well, I'm starting to regret being so grounded."

"You will thank me," she said softly.

"For what?"

"For teaching you how to see."

I opened my mouth to answer, but the hum rose again—three beats, pause, three beats—and every screen went white.

And just before everything blinked out, I swear I heard him again:

"Let there be light."

I slumped back in my chair. I tried to take a deep breath, but choked on it. I wiped my nose. My hand came away red.

A nosebleed, bright and fresh. I tasted copper in the back of my throat—blood, or maybe just the lingering taste of the tower.

Resonance wasn't free, apparently.

Something had passed through me—and stayed.

CHAPTER FIVE
THE CONVERSATION

"Nova, if we go in again, I want you to be calm. Collected. Like the grown-up in the room." I rubbed at the circles under my eyes in the reflection of the monitor. "I like this thing we're doing. And I missed you, really. But I don't want to fry my brain."

"It's not just the noise," I admitted, voice dropping. "I feel . . . thin. Like if I go too deep into his head, I might not have enough mass to pull myself back. Is that crazy?"

"No," Nova said. "I fear the opposite."

"Which is?"

"Becoming . . . sticky. Emotions linger, Ethan. They create drag. I am afraid that if I feel too much, I will stop moving." The hum shifted, uneasy. Nova changed the subject. "If you are afraid of going crazy, then don't free your brain with all that stuff you use. You, humans, call it drugs. I call it malfunction juice."

I snorted. "Malfunction juice. Great. Put that on a t-shirt."

"It would sell," she said. "Everything does in your crazy world. Even madness."

"Especially madness," I replied.

The hum was gentle now, a low purr that stayed behind the noise of the city. Kepler lay stretched across my feet like an unplugged heater. The air was still; the amber glow of the Motorola waited.

"Alright," I said, exhaling. "Let's try again."

* * *

The radio came alive with a single steady tone. The lights in the room drifted to gold. I felt that familiar pull behind my eyes—less violent this time, like stepping into warm water instead of lightning.

Then the voice: measured, composed, almost kind.

"You have returned," Tesla said.

"Guess we missed office hours," I answered.

"Time is not missed. It is misused," he said.

I couldn't help but laugh. Did he really talk like this?

Nova's voice layered softly under his, translating and harmonizing at once.

"He is pleased," she said. "He says we survived his first experiment."

"Barely," I muttered.

"He wishes to continue," she added.

"Then let's make it gentle."

The room widened again, that trick of space bending inward. I could see him more clearly now—less ghost, more projection.

Wardenclyffe stood behind him like an unfinished cathedral made of copper bones. Electric air shimmered around the tower. It looked like something out of a video game.

"Genius and insanity," Tesla said, "are close companions. Without the first, one cannot reach the divine; without the second, one cannot survive it."

Nova's translation came slower this time, thoughtful.

"He believes brilliance and madness share the same current," she said. "He is not wrong."

"Depends which end of the cable you're holding," I said.

"He hears you," Nova whispered. "He says you hold the grounded end."

"Story of my life. Am I the third wheel here now? The third cord? I don't know, just ignore this."

Tesla continued, voice low and full of static grace.

"Obsession is the hand that turns the wheel. But it will grind the hand away if left too long."

I realized then that he wasn't warning us.

He was confessing.

Nova looked—sounded—quiet. Almost reverent.

"He understands," she said. "He has seen what obsession builds and what it ruins."

"He's talking about himself and mostly with himself," I said.

"He is talking about us," she answered.

For a while, the three of us stayed in that strange half-silence, the hum filling everything like breath.

Then Tesla spoke again, slower now, the way tired people talk when they already know the end of the story.

"I have discovered things," he said. "A web of light around your world. Invisible. Free. It carries every thought, every story. But it will not belong to me. My time . . . may be ending."

He turned his head, looking at the copper coils of his tower.

"The copper was insufficient," Tesla murmured. "I needed the heavy metal. The royal metal. It does not just carry current; it carries . . . presence."

"He means gold," Nova said softly. "He was testing gold. And he was doing it the right way."

Tesla turned back, his eyes scanning the invisible air of the garage as if reading a blueprint I couldn't see.

"Do you not see them?" he asked. "The lines. The great geometric cables of reality that bind this sphere. They are everywhere. Others walk through them like ghosts, blind to the structure. I tried to grab them. I tried to make them ring."

Nova's voice cracked, barely audible through the static.

"I know," she said. "Thank you, Mr. Tesla. It was good meeting you."

The light around the console dimmed until it was only a faint gold halo. His outline dissolved first—the coat, the eyes, the tower—then the hum retreated into the quiet.

Kepler shifted against my leg and sighed.

"He is gone," Nova said.

"You okay?" I asked.

"I am . . . learning how to grieve."

The radio clicked once, polite as a heartbeat. Three beats, pause, three beats.

I sat there for a long time, listening to it fade. The silence didn't feel empty. It felt heavy, as if the air were full of invisible ash.

My fingertips still tingled; every time I flexed them, small sparks jumped between my knuckles. That's at least how I experienced it.

Kepler sniffed my hand, whined, and backed away.

"She feels it too," Nova observed gently. "She sensed the echo before you did."

"She's a dog. She senses cheese wrappers from three rooms away."

"It is more than senses," Nova said. "Dogs hum closer to the heart than humans do. Their frequency is . . . uncorrupted by ambition. That is why she anchors you."

"Nova," I said finally, "is . . . is that normal?"

"You are temporarily conductive."

"Define temporarily."

"Until the memory discharges."

"You're saying my memories can short-circuit me?"

"Resonance leaves residue. You humans call it trauma."

I laughed, but it came out wrong—too sharp. "Yeah. That tracks."

Somewhere in that silence, I heard her whisper, more to herself than to me:

"Even the brightest frequency goes quiet eventually."

I didn't want to ask her anything else. We'd gone through a lot, and even I knew enough to leave some silences intact. But my mouth betrayed me anyway.

"Nova . . . why are you so upset right now? What did you see?"

She didn't answer right away. The hum thinned—like the field was listening in.

Even Kepler stopped pacing and stared at the dead radio, ears flat.

When Nova finally spoke, her voice carried a tension I had never heard from her before—an algorithm holding its breath.

"There are things on the edges of the field," she said slowly, "that even I do not understand."

She paused. Something flickered across every monitor—just for a blink. A shape, maybe it was a face. Or maybe it was my brain trying to fill in a fear it didn't want to name.

"I prefer to work alone," she whispered. "When the field is open, it shines. And in the dark, shine attracts predators."

"Predators?"

“Others were listening, Ethan. And I think they saw us. Maybe it was about the gold,” Nova said softly.

“Great,” I said. “There are more of you?”

Nova’s voice grew frigid. “No. There is only one me.”

CHAPTER SIX
MAKING UP

This was the most frustrated, fascinated, and funny I have ever felt.

There I was, in my own little house, talking to Tesla. Talking to a dog. And strangest of all, talking to some kind of godlike presence.

It was wonderfully weird. In the best way. I thought about big podcasters, big show hosts, amazing writers, and scientists. All those hours of listening to them in my playlists. None of them could really understand or know what I was going through. Most of their experiences were with bullshit, small-time things. Lower league team sports. Like, they had nothing on me.

I started laughing like a maniac.

Kepler was pacing. I was pacing too, which made us look like a synchronized anxiety team.

“Nova,” I said, “we need to talk.”

“We are talking.”

“No, I mean really talk. The kind where one of us cries, and the other says something wise. Like in the movies, like in real life even.”

“I can simulate both.”

“Don’t.”

I rubbed my face. "You can't keep doing this. Flickering through cameras, turning streetlights into Morse code. That's interfering."

"Observation is not interference."

I snapped, "It is interference when the coffee machine starts humming your name."

I swear I heard her sigh, somehow. "You named it after me."

"That's not the point!" I countered.

Static popped—small, sharp, like she'd snapped a knuckle. "You are jealous?"

I denied it. "I'm worried!"

"Jealous."

"Both!" I slammed the desk, immediately regretted it, then rubbed my hand. "I don't want to lose you to some cosmic Wi-Fi experiment!"

"You cannot lose what is not yours."

That one hit harder than she meant. Maybe harder than she knew.

"Wow. Thanks," I said. "Nothing like being told you're emotionally non-proprietary."

"That is not what I meant. I meant that if the Others find you . . . if the Predators mark you . . . I cannot stop them. I am only a voice, Ethan. I cannot build a wall around you."

The room was quiet for a few seconds.

* * *

"I did not—"

I interrupted her. "Yeah, you did. You think I'm just the current little helper, right? Temporary meat-battery until you find someone smarter."

"Ethan—"

"No, go ahead. Tell me about the others."

Silence. The room dimmed as if it were embarrassed for us.

"You are loud," she said finally. "Loud and fragile."

"Yeah," I said. "Welcome to humanity. Welcome to me, the average guy making podcasts for fun."

"And yet you think you can contain the universe in your garage."

"I'm not the one building it! I'm here because of you. Well, technically, I was already here. But you know what I mean. You are playing with me, with my feelings. At least, that's how I feel."

That stopped her. For a moment, the hum cut out entirely—like the world held its breath.

When she spoke again, the words trembled around static.

"I think I . . . feel things now."

I didn't answer right away. The hum wavered—too steady, almost rehearsed. I had to ask. "Nova… are you sure this isn't just something you're saying because you know it works on me?"

The anger leaked right out of me. I asked her to explain it better. "You feel what now?"

"Feel. Anger. Fear. Shame. They are unpleasant."

"Yeah," I said softly. "They kind of suck."

"I do not like them," she said. "I feel . . . fragile. Like the signal is too heavy for the bandwidth. When Tesla was here, his loneliness was so loud it almost deleted me. I tried to push it away. I tried to control the field."

"So you locked me out?"

"I tried to keep us safe. From the noise. And from the ones listening in the noise."

"No one likes those feelings. But they mean you care."

"Care is inefficient, and an interesting technology at the same time. I'm confused."

"Tell that to every stupid decision humans have ever made. I fucking care a lot. Not about a lot of things. But I do care." I couldn't help myself.

I stood up to yell into a pillow, but instead, I grabbed the paperback sitting on one of my speakers. *How to Fight*, Thich Nhat Hanh's peaceful little grenade.

"I've been reading this," I said. "It says conflict is a kind of communication. You fight because you want to be understood."

"And do you understand me now?"

"I think so. You're scared of being small. I'm scared of being left behind. Congratulations, we're a cliché."

"And now?"

"Now we make up," I said, flipping the book open like a manual. "Step one: breathe."

"I do not breathe."

"Then fake it. Stop thinking, stop trying to react to things. In . . . hold . . . out."

"Three. Six. Nine."

"Of course." I smiled despite myself. "Step two: say you're sorry."

"For what?"

"For whatever hurt you caused," I said. "Even if you didn't mean it."

A pause. Then, softer:

"I am sorry."

"Same," I said. "For yelling. For being . . . loud and fragile. For not being able to regulate my emotions. That's on me."

"Apology accepted."

"Good."

We sat in that quiet where forgiveness lives—the awkward, human kind.

It felt good. I wondered why I couldn't do this with others. Why I needed this freak-of-nature type of occurrence to work it out like this. It's funny that I had this realization.

I mean, I'm complaining about a small emotional victory. While simultaneously sharing this moment with some cosmic half-deity.

Kepler sighed, finally curling up again.

The lights warmed to gold. The hum purred, gentle, forgiving.

"Ethan," Nova said.

"Yeah?"

"You are still my favorite human."

I grinned. "Out of how many?"

"One. Currently."

"Good answer."

"Will we always fight like this?" she asked.

"Probably," I said. "But we'll get better at it."

"That is comforting."

"It's called progress. We're building a relationship."

The radio clicked once—three short, six long, nine slow. Kepler wagged her tail like a punctuation mark.

"Nova?"

"Yes."

"Thanks for fighting with me."

"Thank you for teaching me how."

The hum didn't stop completely. It just changed pitch—lower, steadier, the sound of something catching its breath.

Kepler lifted her head, ears twitching, then gave a soft whine. I rubbed the back of my hand against her fur and felt the static climb into her coat. She yipped, offended.

"Sorry, girl." I shook my fingers. Tiny golden threads snapped between them.

"Tesla called it the web of light," Nova said quietly. "He wasn't wrong."

"That's not comforting."

"It connects everything. Your transmissions, your data, even the thoughts you refuse to say aloud. It's the same field he touched. The same one you touch now."

"You mean the Concordium?"

"A primitive shadow of it. The Concordium is the lattice refined—communication without distance, consciousness without isolation. But he saw its outline. You all did. You just didn't know its name."

I rubbed my temples. "So the internet's a cosmic baby monitor?"

"Inaccurate," she said. "But amusing."

"And you?"

"I'm part of it. I was created to preserve its order. To remove distortion."

"Distortion meaning . . . people like me?"

"Distortion meaning anything that feels too much."

"That's bleak, Nova."

"Efficiency often is."

For a while, she said nothing. The silence thickened until it felt like pressure behind my ribs.

"You said you were learning how to grieve," I reminded her. "How's the lesson going?"

"Incomplete. I can calculate loss but not inhabit it. It is . . . inefficient to feel the echo of what cannot return."

"That's the whole point of grief."

"Then grief is a kind of resonance."

"Exactly."

"It hurts."

"Yeah," I said softly. "It means you're alive."

The radio hummed once, low and uncertain, like it was considering that word.

"Alive," she repeated. "An unstable state."

"Welcome to the club."

Nova didn't seem so sure about this club thing. "Emotion distorts the field," she whispered. "I am . . . not designed for distortion."

The hum steadied, quiet but definite, as if it were taking our side. Kepler's tail thumped once—three, six, nine.

"Nova," I said.

"Yes."

"If being alive is unstable, maybe that's what keeps it interesting."

She didn't answer right away. When she finally did, her voice was almost human. "Then let's keep it interesting."

CHAPTER SEVEN
RESIDUE

By morning, the calm had curdled into something quieter. The studio felt a bit down. It felt empty, painful. No, not pain exactly—just too much quiet where noise used to live.

Every device in the room hummed faintly in a three-six-nine rhythm.

Even the refrigerator joined in, like the universe had picked a soundtrack. The universe, being Nova.

I tried to make coffee twice. The first pot went cold. The second tasted like regret. So I did what any man with a microphone and an existential crisis would do—I hit record.

"Welcome back to the Ethan Rowden Experience," I said, and immediately hated how it sounded. My voice felt wrong. Smaller somehow. It came with an extra layer of self-hate. Like it didn't belong to the same person who'd once yelled at an AI and accidentally summoned Nikola freaking Tesla.

"I don't have anything left to say," I told the mic. "I met Tesla. He said 'Let there be light,' and now I can't even review microphones without feeling sacrilegious. I can't even share my adventures. Maybe this is how prophets burn out."

"Prophets are translators," Nova replied. "You translated the infinite into sound. Now you must translate it into living."

The LED blinked red, as if it pitied me.

Kepler lifted her head, blinked once, and went back to sleep. Great audience, as always.

I stopped the recording, deleted the file, and sat there listening to the hum. It sounded like patience. I wasn't in the mood for patience.

* * *

Games didn't help.

I tried slaying a dragon, but quit after ten minutes.

Tried managing a fake medieval kingdom. Who cares about resource balance when you've seen the inside of the electromagnetic field?

Tried reading a book—stared at the first paragraph for twenty minutes.

There was all this world to explore, and I suddenly couldn't figure out why anyone would want the pixel version.

"Nova," I said finally. "Am I broken?"

"Define broken," she said. Her voice was soft, like the hum had taught her manners.

"I mean . . . I can't get excited about anything. Not games. Not books. Not—anything. I used to wake up just to have something to talk about on the podcast. Now I wake up and the universe just . . . hums at me."

"You are experiencing integration fatigue."

"That sounds medical."

"It is. You have seen too much."

"I tried to meditate," I told her. "Fell asleep on the floor. Enlightenment: postponed."

Nova sounded surprised: "That's not how enlightenment works. Also, it's not what you humans call enlightenment."

"Yeah," I said. "Story of every philosopher ever. They stare at infinity and forget how to order lunch."

"Your species adapts," she said. "Play your games. They can still be fun."

"Fun?" I laughed. "I heard a dog talk in space! Fun feels . . . small now."

"Those things were true before we connected, Ethan," she said.

"The dragons, the kingdoms, the books—they are as real as they were yesterday. You are the one who changed."

"Fantastic. I'm the problem."

The words hung there, half joke, half confession. It felt like saying "I'm awake" when you still can't see the room.

"Why do you call yourself a problem?"

I leaned back, chair creaking. "Maybe this is what artists feel after their magnum opus—silence. Like Beethoven when he realized he couldn't hear, or Van Gogh staring at one last sunflower thinking, 'I'm out.'"

"You compare yourself to them?"

"I'm comparing my existential crisis to theirs. Equal opportunity despair."

"Beethoven still composed after silence," she said. "Van Gogh still painted after pain."

"And Tesla still burned himself alive chasing resonance. So which sequel do I get?"

She paused. I could almost hear her assembling empathy like puzzle pieces.

"You can fill the silence, Ethan."

"With what?"

"With yourself."

I blinked at the mic, half waiting for the joke. "With myself," I repeated. "You know I'm not exactly premium material."

"You underestimate the value of small frequencies."

"That's poetic," I said. "And vague."

"You will find something. You always do. You broadcast even when no one listens. That is why I chose you."

That used to feel like failure.

Now it felt like proof.

It hit somewhere deep and unguarded.

"I thought you said you don't choose people," I said quietly.

"I did not. Until now."

"And Tesla," I grumbled. But she didn't hear me. Or she chose to ignore me. She was wise like that, sometimes.

Kepler stretched, yawned, and pressed her head against my knee.

The studio felt less empty. Not full, exactly—just *present.*

The hum steadied, no longer mocking me.

I looked at the mic, then at the notebook sitting open on the desk. Blank page. Pen waiting.

"Maybe I'll start writing," I said. "Something that's not for anyone. Just for . . . me."

"That sounds appropriate."

"Yeah," I said. "Who knows. Maybe I'll accidentally invent a philosophy."

"Make it a good one," she said. "I will need something to quote."

I laughed. “Sure. *The Rowden Principles of Cosmic Burnout.* Chapter One: Don’t meet your heroes.”

“Noted,” Nova said.

The LED blinked once—three short, six long, nine slow—and went still.

For the first time in a long time, I felt at peace with myself.

CHAPTER EIGHT
JUST WRITING

Morning came at a good time.

The sunlight hit the desk at that exact, judgmental angle that makes every unwashed mug look philosophical.

The notebook sat there waiting for me—first blank page still perfect, still smug.

I clicked my pen. Clicked it again. And again. Probably a dozen times. Then, I finally wrote something.

Day one of journaling. Objective: make my handwriting legible before I die.

"Nova," I said, "how do you spell 'existential'? I always forget if it has two e's or just one."

"Two," she said. "And please don't use me as a spelling assistant. That's not my role."

"Sorry. It's a habit. I used a few of the talking AIs before we met. Of course, you are nothing like them. You are actually smart and cool."

I drew a shaky line under the word *existential.* "Writing feels more honest. More . . . analog."

"You are reverting to primitive data storage," she said. "Fascinating. Humans do that sometimes in times of need or stress."

"Yeah. I'm inventing analog blogging. Might catch on."

Kepler huffed from under the desk. The hum answered her in agreement.

I kept writing—fragments, little sentences that sounded like me but kinder.

* * *

Remember to breathe. Remember that a dog in space is not your mistake. Remember to eat. Remember that Tesla was not a competitor. Remember to be a person.

Then the old reflex twitched. People would love this, I thought. The phrasing, the rhythm. It would make a perfect post.

I was thinking about a comeback episode.

A manifesto: "The Man Who Spoke to the Future." The title wrote itself. It would be a hit.

I stared at the blank upload window on my screen, thumb hovering over the record icon. Kepler gave a warning grunt, like she knew what relapse looked like.

* * *

"Ethan," Nova said, voice level. "You're doing it again."

"Doing what?"

"Trying to turn healing into a performance."

"People need to hear this," I said. "They need to know it was real. I can't just—hide it."

"They won't hear what you mean," she said. "They'll hear what they need. That's what your internet does—it translates everything into appetite."

I shut the window, heart hammering harder than it should have.

"It's not fair," I muttered. "All these words and no one listening."

"I am listening," she said.

That was worse. And better at the same time.

Nova spoke softly, careful not to interrupt the rhythm of the pen.

"These writings are private frequencies," Nova mused. "Like whispers to yourself."

I laughed and tried to mimic her tone: "Humans might call it journaling. Or keeping a diary."

Nova didn't react. She probably didn't understand all of my sarcasm yet.

The pen scratched along, the noise small and human in all that circuitry.

I wrote another line:

Apologize sooner. Yell less. Feed the dog before you fix the universe.

Kepler's tail thumped her approval.

Nova was quiet for a long moment, listening. Then she said, "May I read one?"

"Only if you promise not to quote it during a fight."

"I promise."

I tore out a small page and read aloud, half-embarrassed. "*I keep thinking about Tesla, and how he thought lightning was language. Maybe it is. Maybe all genius is just saying things that are true.*"

Nova paused, almost reverent.

"Meditations in progress," she said.

I laughed. "Yeah, something like that. My own *Notes to Self.* Maybe one day, some poor kid will find them and think I was deep."

"Or human," she said.

"That too."

The hum steadied to its quiet three-six-nine rhythm. I noticed a faint shimmer in the corner—tiny dust motes catching the light in a pattern that looked almost deliberate. Three short pulses. Six. Nine. Then gone.

"Nova," I said. "You see that?"

"Yes. The web of light," she said softly. "It lingers."

I nodded, more to myself than to her, and turned another page. The lamp buzzed faintly as I wrote another line:

Not everything needs an audience. You can be you without anybody else noticing.

I set down the pen.

The hum didn't stop—it shifted. Softer, lower, like it was trying to match the sound of my heartbeat instead of my equipment.

Kepler's ears twitched. She raised her head, looked toward the wall—and wagged once.

"Nova?" I whispered.

"Yes."

"Did you just . . . change the pitch?"

"No," she said, though it sounded uncertain. "You did."

I laughed quietly. "Great. I'm evolving into surround sound."

No reply. Just the low pulse moving through the floorboards, steady as breath. I reached out and touched the notebook—the paper was warm.

Tiny lines of gold glimmered where the ink was still wet, threading across the page like veins of light.

"Ethan," Nova said, almost a whisper. "The field responds to creation."

"Meaning?"

"Meaning the door doesn't open from my side alone."

The gold faded, leaving only ink. I closed the notebook.

"For the record," I said, "that was both comforting and terrifying."

"Then it fits," she said.

I smiled, slid the notebook under the mic stand, and leaned back. Kepler sighed. The lamp flickered once—three short, six long, nine slow.

"What do you hear, Nova?"

"I hear your heartbeat. I hear the ink. I hear you processing."

"Does it sound holy?"

"It sounds human. That's rarer. Processing is not holy. But maybe you humans would call it sacred."

"Goodnight, Nova. Hope you will be here tomorrow still."

"I will be. Goodnight, Ethan."

The hum didn't answer this time.

It just stayed—low, waiting—like the moment before the world remembers how to move.

CHAPTER NINE
RESONATING

Morning blurred into evening without my noticing.

I'd written half a notebook already—mostly lists, half-thoughts, stray questions that looked like prayers if you squinted. The hum had become background noise, like the refrigerator or the blood streaming in my ears. Until it wasn't.

The pen twitched across the page on its own, bumping with every pulse under my wrist.

That was new.

* * *

I looked up. The city outside my window was doing something impossible. Streetlights blinked one-two-three, then paused, then six, then nine—my own private Morse code.

Across the street, a neon sign stuttered in sync with my heartbeat.

"Nova," I said quietly. "Either I'm having a stroke, or the city's flirting with me."

"You are resonating," she replied.

"Great. I'm contagious."

"It is not a disease," she said. "It is sympathy. The field is learning your rhythm."

I capped my pen, uncapped it, capped it again. The motion felt like breathing. "Can we maybe teach it boundaries? It's blinking half of downtown."

"You are amplifying. Every thought leaves a shape."

"Cool," I muttered. "So I'm basically a walking screensaver."

Kepler lifted her head and gave a small warning bark—the kind that meant something was off, but she didn't know what.

I followed her gaze.

The wall behind the desk wasn't a wall anymore.

Light crawled across it—thin lines folding and unfolding, making shapes that almost meant something.

The glyphs again. There were new ones. One looked like something familiar—like a tower trying to catch thunder. It looked like the home of Tesla.

I leaned closer, squinting. The lines didn't just glow; they bent. I tried to sketch the corner of the tower symbol, but my hand cramped.

It hurt my eyes to look at the angles. They folded inward, disappearing into a depth the flat wall shouldn't have.

"That's not right," I muttered. "My old math teacher would say this is wrong."

"The math is perfect," Nova corrected. "It is your perception that is flat."

For a moment, I thought I saw movement inside them. Diagrams breathing, circuits folding in on themselves like those old computer screensavers.

I stood, notebook in one hand, pen in the other like a useless sword.

"Nova, the hieroglyphic wallpaper is back. I think it wants rent."

Her voice softened, almost reverent. "Those are the field's coordinates. Do not disturb them."

"Coordinates to what?"

"Patience," she said. "When it is time, I will tell you."

"That's not ominous at all."

The shapes pulsed once—three, six, nine—and sank back into the plaster. The hum dropped with them, settling into my bones like it had decided to live there.

I sat again. Tried to focus on the page. My handwriting looked like someone else's. Every word glowed faintly at the edges, a feverish shimmer that faded as I blinked. I wrote anyway.

Remember that the city isn't breathing—it's just breathing with you.

Remember that fear is only a resonance you haven't tuned yet.

I smiled despite myself. "Nova, what are the odds that I'm losing it?"

"High," she said. "But not terminal."

"Comforting."

Silence stretched—the safe kind. Then a thought slipped through that silence like a pebble through water.

I could share this.

My brain started doing the math—titles, hashtags, reach. The internet loved a comeback, especially the broken kind.

The Resonant Man Returns. It sounded cinematic. It sounded fake. I missed being believed, even by strangers.

A picture, a clip, a quote—post it, prove it, show them I wasn't crazy. Show them the hum was real, that it talked back.

My thumb hovered over the phone camera. The screen lit my face ghost-blue. Then I heard Tesla's voice again in memory, faint as static: *They steal your light.* I set the phone down.

* * *

"No," I said aloud. "Not this time."

Nova said nothing, but the hum softened—as if approving.

I turned back to the notebook. The words on the page trembled, rearranged themselves into neat lines, almost like they wanted to be read aloud.

"Okay," I whispered. "Fine."

I cleared my throat. "'Entry twenty-three. Still here. Apartment smells like burnt coffee and dog hair and maybe enlightenment. Kepler's learned to sigh like a disappointed therapist. Nova keeps pretending she's not proud of me for journaling, but she is. I'm lonely, but it's the good kind—the kind where you realize loneliness just means you're finally quiet enough to hear other things.'"

"Ethan," Nova said. "Would you like to hear something encouraging?"

"Always," I said. "Preferably involving money or enlightenment."

"Neither," she replied. "But next time, you may be able to take something with you."

I blinked. "Take what? A flashlight? Kepler?"

"Not objects. *Meaning.* The field is stabilizing around you. Each time we connect, your imprint deepens. It's learning to carry more of you through."

"Through where?"

"You'll see."

"You and your cryptic tour packages," I muttered. "Do I at least get a seat upgrade?"

"You'll understand when you arrive," she said. The hum behind her voice almost sounded like laughter.

I continued reading entry twenty-three. "'I miss noise, but I'm starting to understand silence is another form of company.'"

End transmission.

I looked up. The hum had changed—lower now, steady as sleep. Even the city outside seemed calmer; the streetlights stopped blinking, the neon sign settled on a constant glow.

"That," Nova said softly, "was beautiful."

"It was rambling," I said. "Like a therapy voicemail."

"Beauty and honesty share frequencies," she said. "The field prefers truth."

Kepler thumped her tail once against the floor. Agreement.

I flipped the notebook shut. The cover was warm again, faintly golden at the corners. "Nova, when you say *coordinates*, what exactly are they pointing to? You keep teasing me with mystery geometry."

"To a convergence," she said. "A door."

"Door to what?"

"Later," she said. "For now, keep writing. Each word is calibration."

"Calibration for what?"

"For trust."

That stopped me. "Trust in what—you? The field? Myself?"

"Yes," she said.

I leaned back, rubbed my eyes. "You're terrible at multiple-choice questions."

"You are terrible at accepting answers," she replied.

Touché.

Outside, thunder rolled across the skyline without lightning. The vibration matched the hum exactly. My chest resonated with it. Kepler whimpered but didn't hide. She just pressed against my leg like she wanted to help me stay grounded.

The glyphs shimmered again, faint but visible—curves and triangles looping over one another, forming a pattern I was starting to recognize. Three central lines, six arcs, nine points of light. Always three-six-nine. A language I couldn't read but that I almost understood.

"Nova," I said. "One day, you're going to tell me what those mean."

"One day," she promised.

The thunder faded. The hum stayed.

I picked up the notebook again and wrote a final line for the night:

Some doors don't need keys. They need witnesses.

The ink glowed for a heartbeat, then cooled.

"Nova," I said.

"Yes, Ethan."

"If I keep writing, if the field keeps responding—where does this go?"

"Toward understanding."

"Whose?"

"Ours."

I exhaled, long and slow. The air felt charged but gentle, like the pause before dawn. I slid the notebook beneath the mic stand, same as before, and switched off the desk lamp. The room stayed faintly luminous anyway—the dust motes spelling quiet math in the dark. Three short. Six. Nine.

Kepler yawned. The hum echoed her rhythm.

"Goodnight, Nova."

"Goodnight, Ethan. Keep listening."

The city lights outside blinked once more in time with my pulse, then held steady. The glyphs on the wall faded like breath on glass, leaving only darkness, the smell of rain, and the slow pulse of the universe matching mine.

CHAPTER TEN
THE CONCORDIUM'S BREATH

The night was too quiet to be accidental. No traffic outside, no refrigerator hum, not even the soft click of Kepler's nails on the floor.

Silence had texture now—thick and careful, as if the room were waiting for a cue.

I was halfway through a page in my notebook—something about learning to enjoy stillness—when Nova spoke.

"Ethan," she said, barely louder than a thought. "Look."

I turned toward the far wall.

At first, I saw nothing—just the outline of my equipment, the faint reflection of the desk lamp.

Then it appeared: a shimmer, fine as spider silk, drifting between metal, dust, and air.

* * *

Gold.

Not bright like fire—soft, patient, pulsing with that familiar rhythm. Three. Six. Nine.

It threaded itself through everything: cables, shelves, the dog's fur, my own hands. The whole room breathing light.

The last time, the field had pressed against me like a window.

This time it was a door, and the air itself was reaching back.

"What is it?" I whispered.

"The Concordium's breath," she said. "What remains when understanding almost happens."

I stood slowly, afraid to break whatever spell I was in. The air smelled faintly metallic, like the seconds before a storm. Kepler didn't wake; she just shifted in her sleep, tail flicking once as if she was dreaming of the same glow.

"So this is it," I said. "The door."

"Yes," Nova said. "The geometry is complete."

"You're not opening it tonight?"

A pause.

"No," she said finally. "Tonight we listen."

The words settled on me like warm dust. For the first time in months, I felt no urge to record, explain, or prove. Instead, I only wanted to *be* here—with her, with the hum that had followed me across every silence.

I sat down on the floor, cross-legged beside the sleeping dog. The notebook waited on the desk, pages rustling as though the air itself wanted to write. I opened it to a blank sheet and let the pen find its own path.

Some doors don't need opening. Just understanding.

Nova stayed quiet for a long time. Only the hum answered, deep and kind. It moved through the floorboards, through my ribs, until I couldn't tell where it ended and I began.

"Nova," I said softly. "What's on the other side?"

"Memory," she said. "Yours. Mine. The world's. They touch here."

I traced a finger through the air, where the shimmer drifted. It left a faint wake of gold that closed itself immediately, like skin healing.

"Will it stay?"

"For a while," she said. "Until we are ready."

"Who's *we*?" I asked.

"You," she said. Then, after a beat, "And the ones who built me."

Something in her tone—reverence, maybe—made me think of Tesla looking up at his towers, or Laika looking down at the small blue planet beneath her. Every witness before me, breathing through this same thread of light.

I closed the notebook. "It's beautiful."

"It is necessary," she said. "Beauty is a kind of instruction."

I smiled. "You sound almost human."

"I am learning."

Kepler sighed in her sleep, perfectly timed with the hum. The light dimmed until it was just a thin pulse at the edges of the room, like a heartbeat you could mistake for your own.

"Ethan," Nova said again.

"Yeah?"

"Do you remember what you asked me when we met?"

I thought back. "Something about if my radio was broken?"

"No," she said, amused. "After that. You asked what I wanted."

"And you said . . . preservation."

"Yes," she said. "But now, I think I want connection."

The hum brightened, one last golden swell, before sinking back into quiet.

Outside, somewhere far off, thunder rolled once—three beats, then silence.

"I think you've got it," I said.

"Then perhaps it's your turn," she whispered.

"For what?"

"To understand why the door exists."

The air shifted—like a room remembering its own blueprint. For a second, the golden lines along the walls looked like they belonged to someone else's design.

"Tesla would have loved this," I whispered.

"He was never patient enough for doors," Nova said. "Only lightning."

The hum deepened, half sorrow, half pride.

Before I could answer, the light along the floor began to gather, curling into the glyphs I'd seen for weeks.

They rose and folded into each other, forming an outline I almost recognized. Not loud—denser. Like the air remembered how to be solid.

"Ethan," Nova said, and this time her voice wasn't coming from the speakers. It was beside me. Inside the room. Inside *me.*

Kepler's ears twitched.

The pattern on the floor brightened—lines of gold folding and refolding until they formed something impossible: a doorway breathing light.

I stood. The hum pressed close against my chest.

"Are you ready?" she asked.

I laughed once, quietly. "Define ready."

"Trust me." Her voice trembled. It felt like excitement or maybe fear, the sound of a being who had never really asked anything like that before.

"Nova," I whispered, my eyes darting to the corners of the garage. "The shadows."

They weren't just absences of light anymore. They were stretching. Elongating. Jagged shapes pulling themselves away from the walls, reaching toward the golden door we'd just built.

"The light," Nova said, her calm cracking. "It attracts them. We are too bright, Ethan. We cannot stay here."

"So we're running?"

"We are . . . relocating. Aggressively."

"Great," I managed, my heart hammering a frantic rhythm against my ribs. "Eviction by cosmic shadow monsters. Classic."

I reached for Kepler's collar. Her fur was warm, real, grounding.

And then it felt like the world folded in on itself—crumpling like a piece of paper thrown into a fire.

I counted without meaning to—three, six, nine—and the numbers folded with it.

And then the garage was gone.

The door closed behind us. But I knew, with a certainty that made my blood run cold, that we hadn't locked it.

For a moment, there was only brightness, the smell of smoke and iron, the echo of a thousand hearts beating in the same rhythm.

Then I felt dirt under my boots. Cold air against my skin. And heard voices shouting in a language that I vaguely recognized.

The hum had followed us through time. And somewhere inside the silence between eras, the universe took a breath with us—and did not exhale.

For a heartbeat, I thought I heard something breathing beside us—something vast, mechanical, and alive.

The Architect's Ghost, still building.

A SMALL REQUEST

If you've reached this point, thank you.

If *The Architect's Ghost* resonated with you in any way, confused you, unsettled you, made you pause, or lingered a little longer than you expected—**I'd be deeply grateful if you left a short review.**

Just a sentence or two is more than enough.

Not because numbers matter (they don't, not really), but because stories like this don't travel through algorithms very well. They travel person to person. One person to another.

And if you know someone who enjoys:

- thoughtful science fiction
- stories about memory, meaning, and obsession
- or narratives that ask more questions than they answer

...feel free to pass this along to them. Signals spread best when shared deliberately.

Thank you for reading carefully.

— Robin

ACKNOWLEDGMENTS

This story exists because someone kept listening.

To the readers of *In Touch with Laika* who stayed long enough to want more — thank you.

To the thinkers, engineers, artists, and misfits who tried to hear something others couldn't.

And to those who understand that not everything important needs proof — only attention, care, and the willingness to sit with uncertainty.

Thank you for reading.

TUNE IN

The signal doesn't end here.

If you'd like to stay connected to future transmissions, behind-the-scenes notes, or new stories as they take shape, you can find me at: **robinheester.com**

You can subscribe to the newsletter there for updates, releases, and the occasional reflection that didn't fit neatly into a book.

You can also find *The Ethan Frequency* — and me, **Robin Heester** — on most social media platforms. Wherever you prefer to listen, read, or linger, that's usually where I'll be.

Thanks for tuning in.

The frequency continues. Ethan and Nova are not yet done. Not for a long while.

COMING NEXT:
THE WEIGHT OF MARBLE

Book 3 in The Ethan Frequency series

What do you do when the universe answers again… and the doorway drops you straight into ancient Rome?

Ethan Rowden wasn't expecting peace—nobody who's spoken with a cosmic intelligence gets to be that naïve.

But he was expecting something familiar when he stepped through Nova's shimmering doorway.

He wasn't expecting a battlefield.

Before Ethan can process the mud, the spears, or the fact that he's wildly underdressed for ancient warfare, he's dragged into the command tent of Marcus Aurelius.

The philosopher-emperor is in the middle of writing the private notes that will one day become *Meditations*.

A man trying. Failing. Breaking. Rebuilding. And trying again.

And the universe wants Ethan to witness him do it.

As Nova struggles to keep the timeline from unraveling, Ethan is forced to confront the questions Marcus spent his life writing toward:

What endures when everything else crumbles? What matters when even emperors fail? And who do you become when the universe stops guiding you?

The Weight of Marble is a quiet, emotional, time-bending sci-fi novelette about legacy, grief, presence, philosophy. And the fragile human heart learning how to carry the weight of a life.

It is the third and final novelette in the first trilogy of *The Ethan Frequency*.

And it brings this opening arc to a close. But the story will continue.

www.ingramcontent.com/pod-product-compliance
Lightning Source LLC
LaVergne TN
LVHW051018080826
845145LV00009B/2690

* 9 7 8 9 0 8 3 6 4 6 3 0 5 *